This book belongs to:

Rabbit's Ears

Disney's Out & About With Pooh
A Grow and Learn Library

Published by Advance Publishers

Written by Ann Braybrooks
Illustrated by Arkadia Illustration Ltd.
Designed by Vickey Bolling
Produced by Bumpy Slide Books

ISBN:1-885222-70-X
10 9 8 7 6 5 4

One summer day Rabbit worked in his garden, pulling up weeds.

"Such lovely quiet!" he said to himself. "Every once in a while, a rabbit needs time to think—not about anything special, but just to think. There's nothing quite as nice as a quiet day in the garden."

Rabbit sighed blissfully and tossed another weed onto the pile.

Suddenly the silence was disturbed by a loud buzzing sound. A bee zoomed past Rabbit's head, followed soon after by Pooh. The bear stomped through Rabbit's garden, scattering the weeds.

"Pooh!" Rabbit cried indignantly.

"Sorry!" Pooh called back. "Can't stop! I'm on the trail of some honey."

CABEGE

Rabbit watched Pooh disappear into the forest, then collected the weeds and replaced them neatly in a pile. As Rabbit continued to work in his garden, he began to relax again, and even to smile.

But his smile quickly faded when he heard Roo and
Tigger come bouncing down the path.

"Catch me if you can!" Roo called.

"Here I come!" Tigger shouted back.

Rabbit jumped up. "Please, please, *please* stop making that racket!" he pleaded.

"What racket?" Tigger asked, coming to a halt.

"You're shouting!" Rabbit said, his voice rising. "Can't you bounce without shouting?"

"I guess we can," Roo admitted. "But shouting makes bouncing more fun."

"It's not fun for *me*," Rabbit insisted crossly. "Some of us *like* peace and quiet."

"Then we'll go someplace else," said Tigger. "C'mon, Roo."

After Tigger and Roo left, Rabbit hurried to his toolshed. He found some wood and made a signboard. Then he took out his paint and paintbrush, and in big black letters he painted the words: *Quiet! No Shouting, Talking, etc., or Bothering Rabbit.*

As soon as it was dry, Rabbit carried the sign back to his garden and posted it where everyone would see it.

Quiet!
NO
Shouting
Talking, etc
OR
Bothering Rabbit

The next day, as Rabbit was picking tomatoes, Pooh and Piglet wandered down the path. As they approached, Rabbit could hear them chatting excitedly.

Rabbit stood up and said, "Can't you see the sign? It says 'Quiet! No Shouting, Talking, etc., or Bothering Rabbit.'"

"Oh," Pooh said. "So *that's* what it says."

Piglet gulped and nodded, afraid to speak. Then he and Pooh quietly tiptoed away.

A little while later, Owl came by.
"Why, Rabbit," Owl exclaimed, "what an excellent sign! I should make one for my house."

Quiet!
No
...ting
...ng, etc
...ng Ra...

Owl droned on. "It's awful how some folks never stop talking! Take, for example, my Uncle Robert . . ."

Rabbit tapped his foot impatiently.

"Ah-hmm!" Owl coughed. "I'll be getting along now. Happy thinking, Rabbit!"

Alone at last, Rabbit began picking corn. Suddenly, the sweet silence was interrupted by a loud TAP TAP TAP! Rabbit whirled around, wondering who would dare ignore his sign.

Again he heard TAP TAP TAP!

Finally Rabbit looked up in a tree. "Oh, no!" he said. "It's a woodpecker!"

As the woodpecker continued tapping, Rabbit covered his ears. To his dismay, he could still hear TAP TAP TAP!

Rabbit ran back to his house and dug through his winter clothing. When he found a pair of earmuffs, he clamped them over his ears and said, "This should do the trick!"

But when Rabbit returned to his garden, he could still hear the woodpecker tapping away. The earmuffs were good for keeping out cold, but they were terrible at keeping out loud sounds.

As Rabbit stood in his garden, Eeyore strolled by, crunching noisily on some thistle.

When Eeyore stopped to stare at Rabbit's earmuffs, Rabbit said, "I can hear you crunching!" As he spoke, he glared and pointed to the sign.

Quiet! NO Shouting Talking, etc OR Bothering Rabb

Eeyore carefully read the words. He swallowed the thistle, then said, "I get the message. I won't bother you any longer. Nice seeing you anyway, Rabbit!"

After Eeyore left, Rabbit tore off his earmuffs and marched back inside. "I've had enough noise and bother for one day," he said. "I need a nice, quiet nap."

Rabbit stretched out on top of his bed. But just as he began to doze, he was rudely awakened by a chirping noise.

Rabbit buried his head under the pillow. For a moment there was silence.

Then he heard it again. CRICK-ET! CRICK-ET!

Rabbit jumped off the bed and began searching for the cricket. He finally saw it, but the cricket saw Rabbit first and leaped behind a chest of drawers.

CRICK-ET! CRICK-ET! it called.

"Now I'll never have peace and quiet!" Rabbit moaned. "Perhaps Christopher Robin can help me." And so Rabbit hurried over to his friend's house.

When the boy opened the door, he said, "Why, Rabbit, what's the matter?"

Rabbit sputtered, "Talking. Tapping. Crunching. Chirping. There's too much noise. I just can't think!"

Seeing Rabbit in such distress, Christopher Robin disappeared into the house, then returned with some cotton. "Try this," the boy said.

Rabbit gratefully took two wads of cotton and put
them in his ears.

"Do they work?" Christopher Robin asked.

"What?" said Rabbit.

"Do they work?" the boy repeated.

"I can't hear you!" Rabbit cried.

"Good!" said Christopher Robin as he waved and closed
the door.

That night Rabbit slept peacefully. With the cotton in his ears, he didn't hear a sound.

He didn't hear the cricket chirping beside his bed.

He didn't hear the birds singing in the morning.

And he didn't hear the crows cawing in his garden.

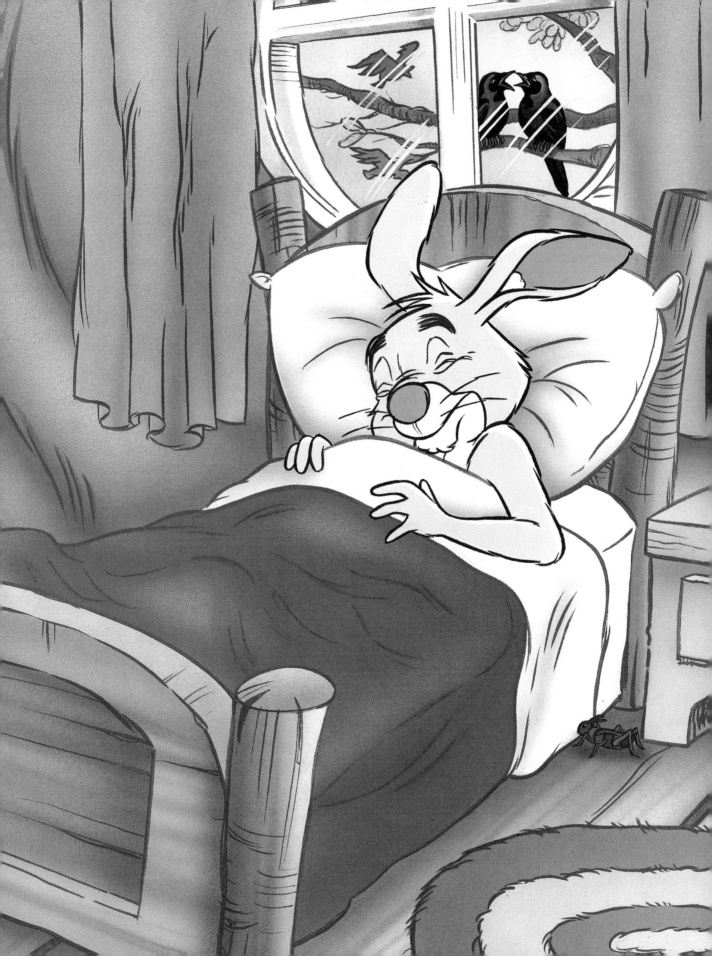

That afternoon, when Rabbit went outside to do his watering, he saw a terrible sight. Every last one of his corncobs had been picked clean!

"Crows!" Rabbit exclaimed. "If only I'd heard them, I could have shooed them away!"

Then, just as he began to clean up the mess, he saw
Pooh and the others walking down the path.

To his surprise, Rabbit's friends walked silently past him.
"Wait!" he cried. "Where are you going?"

Pooh moved his mouth, but Rabbit could not hear him.

"What?" Rabbit said. Then he remembered the cotton balls and took them out of his ears.

"What did you say, Pooh?" Rabbit asked.

"I said, 'I knocked on your door to ask you on our

picnic, but you didn't answer, so I thought you didn't want to be disturbed."

"Oh, dear," said Rabbit, "I wanted peace and quiet, but I guess I went too far."

Then, with an embarrassed smile, Rabbit asked, "May I come on the picnic, too?"

"We're going to make noise," warned Pooh.

"Lots of noise," chimed in Piglet and Tigger.

To prove it, Roo picked up two sticks and banged them together.

"That's all right," said Rabbit. "I'll even help you!"

Quiet!
NO
Zhouting
Talking,etc
OR
BotheringRabbit

Then, as the friends strolled down the path, Pooh made up a song:

Tap-tap, chirp-chirp,
Yakety-yak, clankety-clink.
Poor Rabbit hears so many sounds,
When all he wants to do is think.
But noise can be a lovely thing,
Like friends who laugh,
And birds that sing.

Rabbit smiled and loudly clapped along with Pooh's song.
It was music to his ears!